BEAUTY AND THE BEAST

Retold by MARY

Illustrated by WINS

SCHOLASTIC INC.
New York Toronto London Auckland Sydney

ISBN 0-590-40166-1

Text copyright © 1987 by Mary Pope Osborne.
Illustrations copyright © 1987 by Winslow Pinney Pels.
All rights reserved. Published by Scholastic Inc.
Art direction/design by Diana Hrisinko.

12 11 10 9 8 7 6 5 4 3 2 1   7 8 9/8 0 1 2/9

Printed in the U.S.A.   24

First Scholastic printing, April 1987

To Mary Sams

—M.P.O.

*For the beauty and the beast
in Baba.*

—W.P.P.

ONCE UPON A TIME
there was a very rich merchant.
He had three handsome sons
and three beautiful daughters.
The youngest daughter was the most beautiful.
Everyone called her Beauty,
which made her sisters very jealous.

But Beauty, who was as kind
as she was beautiful,
tried not to mind.

One day the family's house caught fire

and burned to the ground.

Soon after, the merchant found out
that all of his ships had been stolen by pirates!
Beauty's family was suddenly very poor.
They had to leave the city
and move to their small country cottage,
which was deep in a dark forest.

It was very lonely in the forest.
Beauty did all she could to make the best of things.
She helped her father cut wood.
She grew vegetables and made her own clothes.
Her brothers worked hard, too.
But her sisters only complained.

One day a message came for Beauty's father:
"One of your stolen ships has been found,"
the message said.
"You and your partners must come
to the city to collect your fortune."

"Hooray! We're rich again!"
cried the older sisters.

"Thank goodness!" said the father.
"What presents would you like me to bring you from the city?"

"Dresses!" cried one sister.

"Jewels!" cried the other.

Beauty said nothing.

"And you, Beauty, what shall I bring you?"
said her father.

"Nothing, Father. Just come back safely."

"Oh, she makes me sick!" said one of her sisters
behind her back.

"Please, Beauty, you must choose something,"
said her father.

"A rose then, Father?" she said.
"I haven't seen a rose since we moved to the forest."

"*A rose?* Ha! What an idiot!" said her sisters.

But Beauty's father said he would gladly bring her
a rose if that was what she wanted.

Then he kissed his family good-bye,
and started off on the long journey.

When the merchant arrived in the city,
he found that his partners had arrived before him.
They had taken the whole fortune
and left him nothing.
He was still poor.
In sad spirits, he started back.

On the way home,
the merchant got lost in a large forest.
It began to sleet and snow.
The wind blew hard.
The merchant was about to freeze to death
when he saw a light in the distance.

He rode toward the light.
Suddenly the snow and sleet stopped.
The woods were green and filled with flowers.
Birds of every color sang in the bright sunlight.

At the end of the path,
the merchant came upon a great castle
surrounded by beautiful gardens.
In the stable he found oats
to feed his horse.

Then he walked up to the door of the castle
and stepped inside.
No one was home.
In one room, though, a fire was burning,
and a dinner was laid out on the table.
The merchant ate dinner and then went to bed.

The next morning, he found breakfast
laid out on the table.
But still no one seemed to be about.
The merchant ate the breakfast.
Then he went out to feed his horse.
On his way to the stable,
he passed through the garden of the castle.
He saw a beautiful rosebush.
"Oh, at least Beauty will get her rose,"
he said, and he plucked one beautiful red rose.

"Ahhh!" A horrible-looking beast stepped out
 from behind the rosebush.
"What are you doing—stealing my rose?" the Beast yelled.
 The merchant had never seen such a creature before.
 He shouted with horror and fell to his knees.
"Tell me! What are you doing—stealing my roses?"
 yelled the Beast again. "My roses are my prize possession!"

"Oh, I'm sorry! Forgive me! Forgive me!"
 cried the poor man.

"I won't forgive you!" roared the Beast.
"You will die for this!"

"Oh, please, no!" cried the merchant.
"I only wanted one rose for my youngest daughter!"

"You have daughters?" asked the Beast.

"Yes, three. Oh, please, don't kill me—
 for their sake!" said the merchant.

"I won't kill you on one condition,"
  said the Beast.
"You must give me one of your daughters.
  She must come to stay with me
  of her own free will.
  If none of them comes
  before the month is over,
  you must come back yourself.
  If you don't, I will find you and kill you!
  You can never escape from me!"

"All right," said the merchant. "May I go now?"

"Yes," said the Beast. "Take this rose
  and a trunk filled with riches.
  And ride my horse.
  When one of your daughters is ready
  to come live with me,
  the horse will bring her back here."

The merchant did not really believe
any of his daughters
would want to live with the Beast,
but he was anxious to get away.
So he filled a trunk with gold and silver
and climbed onto the Beast's horse
and instantly he was home.

Beauty hugged her father and kissed him,
and her sisters tore open the trunk.
"I have a sad story to tell all of you,"
the father said.
And he told his children about his stolen fortune.
He told them about the snowstorm and the castle
and the Beast.
"So Beauty," he said. "Here is your rose.
I'm afraid it cost me a great deal."

One of Beauty's sisters grabbed the rose
and hit Beauty with it.

"Your stupid rose will kill our father!" she screamed.

"You murderer!" shrieked the other sister.

Beauty wept with shame.

"I didn't mean to cause harm.
  But since it was my fault,
  let me be the one to go to the Beast," she said.

"Oh no, no, no," said her father.

"I must go, Father," she said.
"The Beast will find you
  and kill you if I don't."

  Beauty's father and brothers tried
  to talk her out of going.
  But Beauty was certain her father would be killed
  if she didn't go live with the Beast.
  So one night when everyone was asleep,
  she climbed onto the Beast's horse.

  At once Beauty found herself
  in a cool green forest
  in front of a great castle.
  The trees were lit with a thousand lights,
  and the air smelled of roses.

Inside the castle, a fire was burning,
and dinner was laid out on the table.
Beauty ate dinner and then fell asleep.
The next day Beauty wandered about the castle.
She found a library that contained
all the books ever written.

And she found a music room
that was filled with wonderful instruments
and with singing birds.

When Beauty went back to her room,
she found the table laid out with dinner.
But just as Beauty sat down to eat,
she heard a terrible roar.
The Beast entered the room.
Beauty screamed and hid her face.

"Excuse me," the Beast said.
"Don't be frightened. I only want to sit
 with you while you eat.
 Do you wish me to leave?"

"You are the master," whispered Beauty.

"No, you are now in charge of my castle,"
 said the Beast. "I am only an ugly monster."

 The Beast sat with Beauty while she ate.
 Then he got up and said,
"Good-night, Beauty. Sleep well."
 And he left the room.

 The next day Beauty wandered about the castle again.
 She read books and played music.
 She did not see the Beast until dinnertime.
 Then he sat with her again.
 This time he talked with her about his favorite things—
 his roses, his books, his singing birds,
 and his musical instruments.
 He was very kind,
 and Beauty was not as frightened of him
 as she had been the night before.
 After she finished eating,
 the Beast said, "Good-night, Beauty. Sleep well,"
 and he left the room.

The Beast came night after night to visit Beauty.
She began to look forward to his visits,
for her days were lonely
and she liked talking with him.
One night she said, "I love your company, Beast!"

"How could you?" he said.
"Can't you see I am an ugly monster?"

"No, you are not a monster, Beast.
 Many men are far worse monsters than you —
 for you have a beautiful heart."

"Then will you marry me, Beauty?" the Beast asked gently.

"Oh no, Beast! I couldn't marry you!" Beauty said.

The Beast covered his face
and let out the saddest moan in the world.
Beauty felt sad, too,
but she still could not bring herself
to marry the Beast.

From then on, every night after dinner,
the Beast asked Beauty to marry him.
And night after night, she said no.

The Beast grew sadder each time Beauty said
she couldn't marry him.

One night Beauty dreamed of her father.
Her dream made her miss him very much.
When the Beast came to see her that night, she wept.
"Oh, Beast, I miss my father so much!" she sobbed.
"I wish I could see him again!"

"I will die of grief if you leave me, Beauty,"
the Beast said.

"Oh, please, Beast, let me just go for a visit!
I promise I'll come back in a week!"

"Well, since you promise to return in a week,
I'll give you this ring," the Beast said.
"When you put it on,
you'll find yourself at home.
In one week, put it on your finger again,
and you will instantly be back at my castle."

"Oh, thank you, Beast! You're very kind," Beauty said.

"Remember, Beauty, if you don't come back in a week,
I will die," the Beast said.

"Don't worry, Beast, I'll come back," she said.
Then Beauty put on the magic ring —

and she was home again.

Beauty's father and brothers were overjoyed to see her.
When she told them that she must return in a week,
they begged her to stay with them.
Beauty enjoyed being with her family so much
that when the week was over,
she decided to stay one more day.
When that day was over,
she decided to stay just one more day.

But that night, Beauty had a dream about the Beast.
In her dream she saw he was dying.

Beauty was so upset,
she couldn't sleep the rest of the night.
At dawn Beauty crept into her father's room.
"Father, the Beast is dying," she said.
"I have to go back to him.
I broke my promise. He's very kind, Father.
I don't want him to die!"

"Then go, Beauty," said her father.
"If you care so much for him, return to him."

Beauty kissed her father good-bye
and promised she'd return soon to visit him.

Then she put on the magic ring —
and she found herself back at the castle.
Beauty ran through the castle
calling for the Beast,
but she couldn't find him anywhere.

Finally she ran out to the garden
and found him lying near his rosebushes.
The Beast's eyes were closed,
and he wasn't breathing.
Beauty hugged him and sobbed, "Oh, Beast, don't die!
Please don't die!
I love you, Beast! I'll marry you.
I'll stay with you forever. Please don't die!"

The Beast opened his eyes as Beauty kissed him.

Suddenly Beauty found a prince in her arms.
"A fairy once put a spell on me
  and turned me into the Beast," the prince said.
"The spell could only be broken
  if someone loved me enough to marry me —
  even though I looked like a beast."

So Beauty and the prince had a huge wedding.
Beauty's whole family was invited,

and everyone had a wonderful time —
even her two grouchy older sisters.